The

Dragon
and the Warlord

by

Thomas Bloor

Illustrated by Daniel Atanasov

To my mum

First published in 2008 in Great Britain by
Barrington Stoke Ltd
18 Walker St, Edinburgh, EH3 7LP

www.barringtonstoke.co.uk

ISBN: 978-1-84299-551-8

Printed in Great Britain by Bell & Bain Ltd

Contents

Chapter 1
Dead River

In the first years after the rain stopped falling, the river still flowed. But it wasn't long before the water level fell.

Sheng walked with his father, along the bank. The river was slow and sluggish and the water was a sickly green. Dead fish floated everywhere, flies buzzing around their bloated bodies. The air smelt bad.

"Don't worry, Sheng. We can fish at the river bend where the water's still deep and clean."

They came to a fence built of newly cut logs.

Sheng's father frowned. "This is Lord Zuko's doing."

Lord Zuko lived in a fortress high above the river bend. Each week he sent his soldiers to collect money from the villagers. Some said the money was a tax, which would be passed on to the Emperor. Others said Zuko kept it all for himself. It made little difference to the villagers. One way or the other, their money was taken.

"I won't let Zuko and his thugs starve us to death," Sheng's father said. "If we can't catch fish, we've got nothing to live on. Wait for me here."

Sheng's father climbed over the fence.

The boy waited. After a while he pressed his face against the log fence and peered through a small crack, watching. His father was sitting on the riverbank with his fishing rod in his hands, waiting for a fat carp to swim by.

But it was the riders that came first. Sheng heard the drum of the horses' hooves. He saw his father look up. Zuko and his men arrived in a cloud of dust.

"You dare to take the fish from my river?" said Zuko. He gave a signal to his soldiers. They fitted arrows to their bows. Sheng saw his father lift his fishing rod slowly, and point it at Lord Zuko, as if it were a spear. The horsemen drew back their bowstrings.

"You dare to threaten me, you peasant scum?" said Lord Zuko.

"Yes," said Sheng's father. "I do."

"Then you have made your last mistake," Lord Zuko said.

Sheng heard the hum of bowstrings and the thud of arrows striking home. There was a cry and a splash. Then Zuko and his men were laughing, a cold harsh sound. Sheng turned his face away. He knew his father was dead.

****

Five Years Later

The sun was rising. Sheng stood outside the temple, high up on the hillside, and looked down into the valley. He'd found no fresh grass to take back home with him, though he'd left home long before dawn. Nothing to sell in the market. That meant no money. And no money meant no food and no water.

In the village far below, Sheng could see people, tiny as ants, picking their way up the dusty road that led to Lord Zuko's fortress. He knew that his mother would be among them, clutching her water jar and wheezing with effort as she climbed the dry road in the burning sun.

The warlord's fortress was perched on the edge of a steep cliff. The river used to flow beneath it. But these days there was no river, just a wide channel of bare earth, where snakes sunned themselves amongst the bones of dead cattle.

Sheng gave a sigh. He turned around and walked into the temple. Inside, he stood blinking in the thick, sweet-smelling smoke that drifted through the gloom. On the altar there was a statue of a god, the Great Immortal of the Misty Hills. Sweet-smelling oils, burning in bronze bowls, had been placed before the carving. And yet the stone face still looked angry.

No rain had fallen in the valley for seven years. No matter how much oil was burnt, it would never make the river flow again.

A voice spoke from the shadows.

"One day dragons will fly over the hills once more, and the rains will come."

Tung, the temple keeper, loomed out of the haze. He was an old man, dressed in faded robes. Tung had been going on about dragons and rain for years now. No one took any notice. But today he added something different.

"And you will leave the Misty Hills soon," the old man said. "You know that, don't you?"

"What?" Sheng had never thought of living anywhere else. What was Tung talking about?

"Why do you say that? Even if I wanted to, how could I leave?"

"Ah yes." Tung looked at the ground. "Your mother ..."

"Someone has to look after her. You know she's not been right since Father was ..." Sheng broke off. He still found it hard to talk about how his father had been killed that day by the river, five years before.

"Your mother is stronger than you think," said Tung. "You'll soon find that out."

Sheng blinked. "You don't know anything about us!"

The sweet-smelling smoke from the burning oils stung his eyes and made him choke. He turned his back on Tung and walked out of the temple into the full glare of the sun.

Chapter 2
The Pearl

Many of the village houses were deserted now. Dust and sand blew in through empty doorways. Scorpions scuttled across the floors of silent rooms and snakes slid away into dark corners.

Sheng walked past his uncle Kang's old cottage, and the house where his friend Liu and his family used to live. No one was there any more. Liu and his brothers had left soon after their parents died. Kang had gone looking for water in the hills and had never come back.

Sheng's mother was pouring water from her jar into the barrel by the stove when her son arrived home. The barrel was never even half-full these days. She looked at Sheng's empty backpack as he flung himself down on a seat at the table.

"Nothing?" she said.

Sheng shook his head.

Sheng's mother gave a sigh. "Zuko has put up the price of water again. What with the tax money we have to pay him too, we can hardly afford a jarful a day."

Lord Zuko had been selling water ever since the village well failed and the river ran dry. In the court-yard of the warlord's fortress a well had been sunk deep into the rock. A bucket, lowered into this hole, would take a long, long time to reach the bottom. But when it was pulled back up it would always be full of water. There was an under-ground spring somewhere beneath the fortress. Zuko's soldiers guarded the well day and night. So the villagers had no choice. They either paid Zuko's prices, or they died of thirst. And if anyone protested, Zuko would send out his soldiers, with their swords and their bows.

Sheng stood up and walked over to the water barrel. He peered in.

"Looks like there's a little more water today, Mother."

"Chong-lin gave me some of his supply. Just an extra half a jar. "

"Chong-lin?" Sheng frowned. "Why did he do that? You should have said no, Mother. We're not beggars. I'm sure Chong-lin needs the water just as much as we do."

"He was being kind, Sheng."

Sheng snorted. He strode to the door. "I'm going back out. I have to find something to sell in the market or we'll both starve to death, Chong-lin or no Chong-lin."

"But you've had nothing to eat yet!"

"Then I'll be used to it when we starve to death, won't I?" Sheng said and slammed the door behind him.

****

There wasn't much chance of finding anything he could sell, Sheng knew that. But he needed to be out of the house, away from his mother, away from everyone. Tung the temple keeper had put him in a bad mood and nothing he could do would shake it off.

Before long, he found himself walking along the banks of the dried-up river. In time he came to the log fence where, five years before, he'd watched his father die.

The fence had fallen down. Zuko had no need to keep the villagers away from the river now the fish had all died and the last of the water had dried up. Sheng stepped over the fallen logs. He stood in the place where his father had been killed. He sat down on the baked earth that had once been the river-bed and he put his head into his hands. He sat that way for some time.

When he looked up again he could see a patch of vivid green grass, tall and lush, waving its seed-heads in the gentle breeze.

Sheng stared. He rubbed his eyes. It was really there. Out in what had once been the middle of the river, beyond a heap of dusty pebbles and the rotting timbers of an old fishing boat, there really was a patch of fresh grass. He hadn't seen anything as green as that for months.

There was no one else in sight, but still Sheng ran fast across the dry river-bed to the place where the grass was growing. He fell to his knees beside it, held out his hands and let the grass blades ripple through his fingers. The earth around the grass roots was damp and soft. Sheng dug into it with a stick he'd found. If he could uproot the patch of grass without damaging it he could take it back home and plant it behind the house. Then he and his mother would have a constant supply of fresh grass to grow and sell in the market.

Gently, he eased the tangle of stems out of the ground. A sprinkling of earth fell from the long stringy roots. Then something else dropped down into the hole where the grass had been. Something pale and round and shimmering.

A pearl! It was a pearl. Sheng picked it up. He held it between finger and thumb and lifted it close to his face. The pearl was a real beauty.

"I can't believe it," Sheng whispered to himself. "First the grass, and now this."

He stowed the clump of grass away in his pack, and hid the pearl down among the green stems. Carrying his new treasures on his back, Sheng went home.

Chapter 3
In the Water Barrel

"What should we do with the pearl, Mother? Sell it?"

"No, Sheng. Let's keep it, for now at least. We may need it later. Give it to me."

Sheng placed the pearl in his mother's hand. She held it there for a moment, studying the way the light fell on its smooth round surface. Sheng remembered what Tung had said about her. Perhaps the old man was right. She did seem stronger these days.

Sheng watched as his mother took the pearl over to the water barrel, lifted off the lid and dropped it in.

"There," she said. "It's hidden."

So the pearl stayed in the water barrel while Sheng and his mother carried the clump of fresh grass outside and planted it carefully in a shady spot close to the back door. They both knelt on the ground and patted down the earth around the plant with their bare hands. But already the grass had begun to wilt a little.

"It needs water," said Sheng.

His mother went into the house. Sheng heard her gasp.

"What is it?"

"Come and see," she said.

"What has happened?"

Sheng hurried inside. His mother pointed at the water barrel.

"What's the matter?"

Sheng lifted the lid. Water slopped over the edges and trickled down the wooden sides, forming small pools on the floor. The barrel was full to overflowing with clear, cool water.

"How has this happened?" asked Sheng. "Last time I looked the barrel was more than half empty."

Sheng looked at his mother. She shook her head slowly.

"Your friend Chong-lin hasn't sneaked in and given us all this water, has he?" Sheng asked.

Again, Sheng's mother shook her head. "Chong-lin is a generous man, but even he couldn't afford to give away so much," she said.

"Then I don't understand."

They stood for a moment, in stunned silence. Sheng's mother picked up a jar and dipped it into the water barrel.

"Careful!" said Sheng, watching the water running down the side of the barrel. "You're spilling it!"

His mother looked at him. "Sheng," she said. "I think I know what has happened. Tung, the temple keeper, once told me that sometimes, in a place where a dragon once lived, a special pearl can be found, buried in the earth. Here in the Misty Hills there have been no dragons for a very long time. That's why we are so often cursed with no rain for years on end and why we all starve. It's because we don't have dragons any more to breathe rain clouds into the air. This pearl you have found must be all that's left of the last dragon to live here. You've found a dragon's pearl. Such a thing can be truly magical."

"Magical? Mother! Tung is an old man. Some of his stories are ... well, they're just stories."

"Then how do you explain this?" Sheng's mother was pointing at the water barrel. "I just filled the jar. You watched me do it. And yet now the barrel is full once again."

Sheng stared. It was true. The barrel was so full, water was trickling over the brim and running down the sides.

Sheng and his mother watered the grass they'd planted at the back of the house. But by the following day, the grass had withered and died. The ground was too dry and parched and the roots could not take hold. Inside the house, however, the water barrel remained brim-full, no matter how many jars or pitchers they drew from it.

"We should give water to the other villagers," Sheng said. "It isn't fair that they have to beg Lord Zuko to sell them a drop or two from his musty old well."

"I thought you didn't approve of giving water away for nothing, Sheng," his mother said. "After all, the villagers aren't beggars!"

Sheng smiled. "This is different." He stepped out of the back door and looked along the valley towards the steep slope that led to where Lord Zuko lived. He could see the walls of the fortress, stark against the sky.

Chapter 4
Night of the Riders

So Sheng and his mother began giving water away by the bucketful. Soon the villagers all had plenty to drink, with enough water left over to cook with, and to wash themselves and their clothes. And they also had water to pour onto their gardens so they could grow fruit and vegetables once again. No one needed to carry a water jar and a handful of coins up the road to Lord Zuko's fortress anymore.

One hot afternoon, Sheng had been helping Tung sweep the temple and lay fresh flowers in front of the statue of the Great Immortal. Now they were sitting outside in the sun, the old man in his robes and the young man in his wide-brimmed hat.

"You of all people should know what a terrible enemy Lord Zuko can be," Tung said.

"I know what Zuko is," said Sheng.

"He wants to know where the people are getting their water from."

"Why should he care? Three times since I found the dragon's pearl, Zuko has put up the price of the tax we have to pay him. So he still gets his hands on as much of our money as he ever did."

"Ah," said Tung, "but he does not have quite the same level of power that he used to have. He wants to know why the villagers no

26

longer need his water. He is puzzled. His puzzlement makes him angry. And when he is angry, we are all in danger."

"Well, anything that makes Zuko unhappy is fine by me," Sheng said.

"Even though he will soon find out the truth?"

"Why should he?" asked Sheng. "No one will tell."

"Someone will. In the end, someone will. Lord Zuko will push the village to the limit. Already he has sent his soldiers to burn houses and destroy crops. He is a ruthless man, as you know. In the end, someone will tell him about the dragon's pearl."

"But I never talk about it. No one knows we have the pearl."

"I do," said Tung.

"Well, yes, but ..."

"And your mother knows. And Chong-lin."

"Chong-lin!"

"And many others, too," said Tung. "Lord Zuko will find out, and when he does, he will come with his soldiers to take the pearl for himself."

Sheng was silent for a moment. Then he gave a sigh and shook his head. "I will not allow it. Whatever else happens, I will not let Zuko take the dragon's pearl."

Tung said nothing. He just looked at Sheng and slowly nodded his head.

****

It was less than a week later that the riders came. They came in the dark hours after midnight. Sheng woke to the thunder of hooves. He knew who it was and what they wanted. Tung had been right. Lord Zuko had come for the dragon's pearl.

Sheng lay in the dark, frozen with fear. Out on the road, he heard the soldier's horses snorting and stamping their hooves.

Heavy boots tramped up the path between the beds of lush grass that now grew around the house. There was the clank of armour, the creak of leather, the hiss of swords being drawn.

Sheng got up and moved silently through the shadows to the kitchen where the water barrel stood. He could hear Zuko's soldiers moving to surround the house and to cut off any chance of escape. There was a sudden, violent pounding at the door.

"Open! In the name of Lord Zuko!" a harsh voice called out. "Open at once!"

Sheng's mother came into the kitchen with a lamp in her hand. There was fear in her eyes.

"What should we do?" she said.

Sheng said nothing.

"Perhaps, if we let them in, they'll think we've got nothing to hide and –"

"And butcher us anyway," Sheng cut in. "No, Mother," he went on. "Let's not make it any easier for them. These are the same men that killed Father, remember."

There was a great crash and the sound of wood cracking as the door was kicked in. Then the soldiers were all around them, the plumes on their helmets brushing against the roof beams.

One of the men stepped forward. He was shorter than the rest, and was dressed in rich silks. His armour was covered in images of demons and monsters. He held a thick-bladed sword in his hand. It was Lord Zuko.

"You!" he said, pointing his sword at Sheng's mother. "You have something here that I want. A certain magic pearl. I demand you hand it over at once. It is my due as lord of this region!"

Sheng's mother took a deep breath. There was a strained silence. Then she let out a loud shout. "The rice jar, Sheng! Don't let them look in the rice jar!"

In spite of the danger they were in, Sheng almost laughed out loud at his mother's simple trick.

Lord Zuko smiled. "These villagers are so stupid!" he said. "The pearl is in the rice jar! Find it!"

The soldiers swept all the jars from the shelves. The heavy pots smashed into pieces as they hit the ground. Rice, grain and dried beans were scattered across the floor. No one was looking as Sheng turned to the water barrel. He pushed off the lid and thrust his arm deep into the cool, fresh water. He felt his fingers close on the dragon's pearl.

But then he heard one of the soldiers scream out, "Look! The kid's got the pearl!"

Lord Zuko spun around and stared at Sheng, a look of utter fury on his face.

"Do you dare to defy me?" he said.

"Yes," said Sheng. "I do." And he tipped back his head, dropped the pearl into his mouth and swallowed it.

Chapter 5
Blood and Skin

"You're going to regret that, boy!" Zuko said. He nodded to his soldiers. "Hold him fast. I'll gut him like a fish. I will have that pearl!"

Sheng fell to his knees. The soldiers moved in to grab him but then they stopped and stared. What was happening?

Sheng's mother stepped forward. "Sheng? What's the matter, son? What is it?"

Sheng clasped his hands to his throat. He could hardly breathe. There was a strange red glow coming from between his fingers. It lit up the horrified faces of the soldiers, of Lord Zuko, of his mother, reaching her hands out towards him. The glow moved down, into his chest. It was as if a powerful light was shining through his rib cage, out through the layers of muscle, out through his blood and his skin. The pearl was burning as bright as the sun as it slipped down into his belly.

And then the pain hit him. He bent double with a cry of agony. He felt as though a red-hot coal had been planted in his gut. The burning spread through him, as if the blood pumping through his veins was suddenly scalding hot. Sheng screamed again and again.

The soldiers backed away.

"Take hold of him!" ordered Zuko, but he too took a step back. Only Sheng's mother

remained, both hands reaching out to hold her son as he kicked and twisted in agony.

"What's happening?" Her voice rose to a wail.

Sheng's skin was shining with sweat. Steam rose from his body. He threw back his head and arched his back, howling and moaning. Another sound, even more awful than Sheng's cries, now filled the air. It was the crackling of bone and flesh as some terrible force caused Sheng's body to stretch and bend.

He could feel his ribs shift and his spine grow longer, pulling at his neck and his limbs, changing his shape forever. His shrieks and yells grew muffled and distorted as his jawbone thrust forward and rows of jagged teeth pushed up through his gums. His mother was still holding his hands in hers.

But now Sheng's hands were swelling up. Curved claws burst through his fingertips. He pulled away from his mother and curled into a tight ball, coiling his body around itself as his skin thickened into a tough and scaly hide.

When next he opened his eyes, Sheng was alone with his mother.

"Lord Zuko is gone," she said. "He's run away back to his fortress with all his brave soldiers shaking with terror."

Sheng opened his mouth to speak. Steam billowed from between his jaws, but he found he couldn't say a word.

"Don't try to talk, Sheng. I don't think you can anymore. Everything is changed. We have nothing to fear from Lord Zuko. He is afraid of you now. Do you know what you have become, my son? You have turned into a dragon. A magnificent water dragon."

But Sheng had no time to wonder at what had happened to him. His brief moment of peace was over. The fire that the pearl had started in his belly now flared up once again. He needed water to soothe the burning inside, and he knew he wouldn't be able to control the terrible craving he felt.

His mother seemed to sense that something was about to happen. She stood back, watching, as Sheng lifted his head, stretched out his long serpent's neck and pressed his coils against the ceiling. Sheng saw his mother throw herself back against the wall. A great shudder ran through him. It was time to go.

In one lightning-quick movement, he burst out through the broken doorway and flew up into the night sky. His glowing scales lit up the darkness. A pair of powerful wings spread out at his back.

Sheng's nostrils widened as he drank in the night air. Somewhere close by there was water in this dry land. The people in the village had their water barrels. But that would never be enough to satisfy the thirst Sheng felt growing inside him. There was only one place where he could truly drink deep. And that was the well at Lord Zuko's fortress.

Sheng flew close to the ground, following the sloping road. The walls of the fortress stood out, black against the silver glow of the moon-light. He could smell the water. His dry throat and burning belly cried out for it. Sheng beat his wings and rose up, high above the land. He looked down on the highest peaks of the Misty Hills, on the fortress and the dry river bed far below. He hung for a moment in the still night air. Then, like a thunderbolt, he fell upon his enemy.

A swarm of arrows rose to meet him as he swept down over the fortress walls. But the shafts just bounced off his leathery skin and clattered to the ground, no more deadly than an armful of dried twigs.

Sheng let out an angry roar, scorching the wall tops with a burst of his steamy breath. At this Lord Zuko's men threw down their bows and ran. They fled blind, running out into the night, leaving the fortress gates wide open behind them. Snorting in panic, the horses in the court-yard broke free of their tethers and they too thundered out of the gates and away. Sheng the dragon circled in the dark air above the castle, watching. Only Lord Zuko was left inside the fortress.

Chapter 5
Dragon's Farewell

Sheng flew in through the open gates and followed the scent of cold spring water. He slithered on his belly down a long flight of stone steps and came to a chamber. There was Lord Zuko, standing by his prized well.

Sheng gave a low growl. Zuko let out a howl of pure terror, dropped his sword and ran. Sheng watched as the warlord leapt out of a window and scrambled down onto a ledge in the cliff above the river. He was

trying to hide behind the stump of a long-dead mulberry tree.

Sheng turned away with a snort of disgust. He dived into the well, pushing his way down to the spring, deep inside the cliff. He plunged his head into the cold, dark water and drank. He drank and drank, turning and twisting, his thrashing coils splitting the rock all around him. He drank and drank and drank.

At last he'd drained the spring dry. Sheng was no longer thirsty. He dug his way out through the soft earth at the base of the cliff and burst into the light. He found himself in the dry bed of the old river.

Voices called his name. Sheng looked up. The sky was alight with what seemed like hundreds of glowing dragons, blazing like comets in the darkness.

"Sheng! Sheng! Join us!" the dragons sang.

Sheng spread his wings and took to the air. As he flew with the dragons he knew he was among his own kind. They had come for him.

One by one, the winged beasts began to let out great gusts of steam. The steam built into clouds that soon filled the sky from horizon to horizon. Sheng joined in, adding his own steam to the growing storm. He followed his fellow dragons as they circled and swooped, whipping up a wild wind with the beating of their leathery wings.

At last the storm broke and, for the first time in seven years, rain poured down onto the Misty Hills. It rained and rained as if it would never stop.

****

Crouched down behind the tree stump in the pouring rain, Lord Zuko watched the dragons circling above him. He couldn't fight

dragons, he knew that. But they wouldn't stay for long. When they were gone, he would go back to his fortress, round up his soldiers, and start all over again. And the first thing he'd do would be to kill that annoying woman, Sheng's mother, whose son had denied him the magic pearl.

Just as he was thinking these happy thoughts the warlord heard a noise from somewhere on the cliff above him. It was a mighty booming sound. He looked up. There was his fortress. But it was coming towards him.

It was the last thing he ever saw. The damage Sheng had done deep beneath the cliff, and the effects of the sudden downpour of rain after so many dry years, had caused the cliff to crumble and collapse. Lord Zuko, together with the falling stones of his fortress and the broken rocks of the cliff-face, plunged screaming into the river and was no more.

Sheng lay in the surging waters. The storm had been so fierce that the river had not only filled up, it was now in danger of bursting its banks. Rain still fell, but it was gentler now.

A woman stood on the river bank, the water lapping around her ankles. It was Sheng's mother.

"You mustn't worry about me, Sheng." She smiled at him. "You've taken care of me for long enough. I have good friends here in the village. Chong-lin will look after me. Now you must go. This place is too small for you. Follow the dragons, Sheng. Go with them to a new life."

The current was pulling Sheng down the river. Up in the sky, the glow from the departing dragons was already growing faint. Sheng turned to look back at his mother. As he did so his wings cut into the bank, scooping out a great curve of sand and earth. Water rushed into this new bend in the river.

"Whenever it rains, Sheng," called his mother. "I'll know you're up there, flying over the Misty Hills!"

Sheng turned again and his wings cut another curve in the river bank.

"Goodbye, Sheng! Goodbye, my own boy! Goodbye! Goodbye!"

Sheng turned back again and again, cutting a new twist in the river at every turn, as he drifted further and further away. He looked back at his mother with sorrow in his eyes. But the river swept him along, following after the dragons as they left the Misty Hills behind them. They were starting the journey to their distant Kingdom, a place no human could ever set foot.

Sheng's mother stood on the riverbank, waving, long after he had vanished from sight. Then she turned back to the village and saw Chong-lin waiting for her.

****

Many years have passed. The river is full again, but little seems to have changed in the Misty Hills. There is still an old man in faded robes tending the temple, high up on the slopes. But if you look closer, you'll see that the river flowing beneath the crumbling, empty cliffs now has a great many twists and turns in it, as it flows out across the valley.

And inside the temple, there is a different statue on the stone altar. It's a brightly painted carving of a great winged water-dragon, its breath a billow of clouds. This dragon is clearly a creature of great power. And yet there is a single tear, glistening in the corner of its eye.

Barrington Stoke would like to thank all its readers for commenting on the manuscript before publication and in particular:

Daniel Fraser
Mathew Robertson
Andrew Wall
Sharon Wall

Become a Consultant!

Would you like to give us feedback on our titles before they are published? Contact us at the email address below – we'd love to hear from you!

info@barringtonstoke.co.uk
www.barringtonstoke.co.uk

BATTLE CARDS

Thomas Bloor

Author

Favourite hero:
The Shoveller from the film Mystery Men.

Favourite monster:
David, the werewolf from the film
An American Werewolf in London.

Special secret power:
I am able to withstand any amount of
pain.

Favourite fight scene:
Where Maximus fights the emperor at
the end of the film Gladiator.

Goodie or Baddie?
A goodie who used to be a baddie.

RELOADED

WHO WILL WIN?

Daniel Atanasov

Illustrator

Favourite hero:
I like huge characters like Potemkin
(Guilty Gear Arcade Game).

Favourite monster:
Tessai, one of the five devils who
destroyed the Koga ninja clan (Ninja
scroll).

Your weapon of choice:
Something heavy like a two handed
sword or a war hammer. There are too
many to chose only one!

Special secret power:
My venom

Goodie or baddie:
I've always wanted to be the good guy.
But I never am :(

RELOADED